THE FALL OF NAQUINN

Zining Fan

For my parents, who kept me going and supported me every step of the way.

For my mentor, Hannah Page, who gave me great advice.

Contents

Prologue

It was a dark night with nothing but a faint sliver of a silver moon setting partially hidden behind the dark gray clouds. The mist was thick that night. It pressed on the shoulders of a lone figure walking away from a burning wreckage, which resembled a little log cabin on top of a hill surrounded by a forest. But if you looked more closely you would see that the one shape was a mother carrying a two-year-old child and that they were fleeing from the burning wreck that was their house. They trekked towards the city that was not far away yet seemed impossibly so. Not long after they set out the baby had started to cry and pointed to the direction of the city and said his first word he ever said in his life, "No."

"But we have to go there," the mother said.

"No!" the baby insisted and started to cry even harder. The mother ignored the protests and just kept going, unaware of the danger ahead.

Elsewhere, Naquinn, the prince of darkness, was plotting evil things with his huge monster, a king cobra who was three feet wide and one hundred feet long. Its name was Siskilinth Naga and it was given by Rahmal, the king of darkness, to Naquinn. It was truly a creature from nightmares with those slitted black pupils looking like they could stare down anyone until they melted into a puddle of darkness. It had lean rippling muscles and fangs that dripped with viscous black venom. Naquinn was not much better looking, though he was half-human and half-demon. His skin was shriveled up beneath his hood; his face was pure white and his eyes were black. Gazing into its eyes you would see a dark pit that could only be filled with desires of the past, the present, and the future.

"I will first kill the mother and torture the son. After that, I will unite with my father and take down the sun, the moon, and the stars. And then the world will only see darkness and every light will be extinguished," He said to Siskilenth. Then he and Siskilenth disappeared in a swirl of darkness.

He and the cobra appeared right in front of the mother and the child as they were nearing the city. They screamed and the mother ran at the sight of the huge cobra. Then Naquinn said to Siskilenth, "Kill the mother, not the boy, but bring him before me." As Siskilenth hurried to do his bidding, Naquinn brought out his scythe. Siskilenth ate the mother by swallowing her in one swift gulp and brought the boy before Naquinn. "Hahahahaha," Naquinn cackled, "you are mine now, boy." He used his dark magic to make a jagged black knife to scar the boy on the cheek. Then he summoned something with a gesture of his hands. It was a sphere, a dark orb of something. If you looked closer you could see that it wasn't a dark sphere. It was a flock of something sharp, a flock of knives that raced toward the boy..

1. A Good Day

I had been having that nightmare for weeks. Every time I saw that creepy orb of knives, I woke up. "Magus," Mom called, "breakfast's ready, come quickly."

"Alright, I'm coming," I whined, irritated that my mother wasn't letting me sleep a few more minutes. It was only six-thirty and school didn't start until nine.

"What's wrong, mom?" I asked, "can't you see it's only six-thirty?"

"Yes, I see it's only six-thirty!" she snapped. "And I see a boy who is going to be late for his skiing competition if he doesn't wake up right now."

"What? I thought today is Thursday," I yelled down.

"Well, what you thought isn't what it is, and always observe before you think."

Thirty minutes later, we were at the

competition.

The racetrack was a 1-mile 75-degree slope. The announcer was a stout man who said everything with enthusiasm. The first person that went down the slope took 45.59 seconds. The second person took 47.84 seconds and so on and so on. Finally, it was my turn. The best time had been 44.41 seconds. "Magus Diamond!" the announcer stated, "at age 15 he will be the second to last person you will see ski today. He has won other races before. 3...2...1... GO!" With the wind behind me and the snow in front of me and going over 80 miles an hour, I felt pure joy. I charged down the slope and crossed the finish line. At the same time, the person with the timer gently squeezed it. And then the person with the timer announced, "Beating everyone so far, Magus Diamond with a perfect 36.00 seconds." The crowd went nuts. The last person got a good 41.37 seconds. Then the announcer said with his enthusiasm, "In first place, going gold with a perfect 36.00 seconds, Magus Diamond." The crowd cheered as the medal was placed around my neck.

"In second place...," said the announcer. But my mother led me away before I could hear anything else to congratulate me and send me to school.

With those brown eyes, that black hair, and that understanding smile, my mother was undoubtedly the nicest person in the world-- although she did infuriate me sometimes she had said and taught me stuff that normal fifteen-year-old students should know about. "You did so well, Magus, you got 36.00 seconds. As a reward, you get a slice of cake and some hot chocolate, and extra horse riding lessons from me," she said, leading me toward the car. So she bought me a hot chocolate and a slice of cheesecake at the coffee shop then drove me to school. It was 10:30 am when I was dropped off at school. The front office let me in and I headed for my classroom. I said Hi to my friend Alex Geode. He was a fifteen-year-old boy with black eyes, dark hair, and a smile that was always there.

"Where were you this morning?" he asked.

"I was at the skiing competition, remember?" I said.

"Oh right, did you win something?" questioned Alex.

"Oh, I won the gold medal, some hot chocolate, and a muffin," I said.

Then Alex asked me, "do you want to play chess at the park tomorrow?"

"When?" I asked.

"Ten," he said. The rest of the day went by without much else except for the fact that in science I found a manila envelope and when I opened it it had a piece of paper in it. The paper said, Meet me in the park at ten in the morning Saturday. No delays. Bad people are coming for you. Do not tell your mom about this. That was all the note said. I wanted to tell Alex about it but I was afraid that it was a prank. Still, I had to make sure. I spent the rest of the day thinking about the note. I had a few theories about it. The likeliest theory was that it was a prank, but then what was going to explain the weird dreams I was having? At that moment, I made up my mind. I was going to the park tomorrow morning at ten. I was thinking about it even as I drifted back to sleep.

2. The Betrayal

I woke up suddenly from the nightmare. I was so frustrated it wouldn't show me more. It was still the same. The nightmare and the note I really felt were connected somehow. I glanced at my alarm clock; it was already nine twenty-five. I went downstairs and found my mom cooking. "Good morning, Magus," she said.

"Morning Mom," I replied, "I have to check something out at the park after breakfast." My face darkened for a moment and my mom saw the change of expression immediately.

"Magus, is something wrong?" she asked.

"No," I lied. "I just have to check on something then play chess with Alex." So I had a quick breakfast and rode toward the park. It was exactly ten when I arrived. I saw that Alex had already arrived and sat at the table we usually sat at. The funny thing was that he wasn't carrying chess supplies. He looked ready to go somewhere.

He waved me over and said in a hushed voice, "We must leave immediately."

"Why?"

"Because bad bad people are coming after you!"

"You are lying."

"I am not! And I am a unicorn."

"How?" I asked flatly. Inwardly I thought, *well I'll just lose a crazy friend.*

"I am one."

"Fake."

"I am not a fake."

"Prove it!"

He pulled me away into the woods and a magical thing happened. He pulled out a horn. The horn was not what you would expect from a narwhal horn or any other horn. It was a horn filled with a rich dark energy. I could feel my eyes being drawn to it. I could feel it sucking the sunlight in. Alex mumbled something, disappeared into a black swirl and transformed into a stallion with one horn and a coat of fur that was as black as night mixed in was a little pearl white that glittered. I could tell that the black was trying to eat away the white. The horse stood half a neck above me snorted, whinnied once and transformed right back and stumbled down clutching his stomach and asked in a wheezy voice, "Now do you believe me?"

"I'm dreaming."

"No, you're not."

"But unicorns are magic and magic is not real."

"Well, unicorns and magic are both real."

"But unicorns aren't real," I said. "And I still have to get back to my house to go tell mom about this."

"But there is no time and I know a very fast way if you trust me."

"How fast?"

"Very fast."

"Fine. Show the way."

After that, he transformed back into the unicorn and stamped his hoof six times and a staircase appeared. The staircase was not an ordinary staircase. Rather, it opened up from the ground and went down. It was made of obsidian and that was so dark that I could literally see the light being sucked into it. When we descended I saw a huge castle made of black stone that looked menacing. When Alex led me in, I knew that I had made a big mistake in trusting him and coming with him to this hideous place. The castle smelled like rotting flesh once we were inside. Then the room's temperature dropped and a cold voice from the darkness said, "Welcome to my castle and your final resting place."A hooded figure flicked his hand in the torchlight and I doubled over and instantly fell asleep…

3. An Unexpected Ally

The same dream. But only this time it showed more. Suddenly a ray of sunlight vaporized the knives as if they had never been there. Naquinn gave a frustrated yell and drew another knife. It was nothing like what you would ever expect from a knife. It was a jagged blade and it was so dark that if you gazed into it for more than three seconds it would start sucking the soul from you. It was a weapon of pure evil. Just as Naquinn thrust his knife down, a beam of blinding light swallowed it. Then a booming voice said, "Leave my son alone, the police will be here soon and even you are no match for the guns they have because I have alerted them."

Then Naquinn whispered in a slithery voice, *We will deal with this later,* and he and the snake vanished into a pool of darkness.

My eyes opened. I could see only by the dim glow of the torches that pooled through the bars. Bars? Where was I? What was I doing here? Then I remembered with dread I was in a cell in some castle. I heard footsteps coming toward my cell. I froze and silently drew the pocketknife that I always kept in my pocket. It was a finely carved piece of wood hugging cold titanium. The blade itself was a finely crafted four inches that gave off a blue glow. It cut through wood as if it were butter. My mom had given it to me for my ninth birthday and had said to keep it safe and never let it out of sight. But what about school? I had asked her but she had said even in school keep it in your pocket. So she had probably meant it for this. The footsteps were nearing and it was time to do something about it. I hid the knife behind my back. I was going to kill whoever was just turning the corner. He walked right into the light that briefly illuminated his face. It looked nightmarish, like an orc from a *The Lord of the Rings* movie, but it had red eyes. Just as I was about to stab it, it transformed into a? Centaur? And it spoke. Its voice was deep and resonant. It said, "Point that hilliu away from me."

"What did you say? Hilliu?"

"That knife in your hand is not a regular knife."

"Of course it isn't a normal blade, it gives off a bluish glow."

"The truth is much more interesting than it seems, but I have no time to explain because--" He was abruptly cut off by the sound of footsteps coming toward the cell, my cell. The centaur transformed right back to the goblin and then the person turned the corner. He looked a little worse than the last time I had seen him but I'd recognize that face anywhere and anytime. "You," I snarled.

"Yes, me," he said, sounding a little smug. *Come a little closer*, I thought. So I asked him a question.

"Why did you do this?" I asked him.

"Because I was tired of being a pawn for the Blinding Light Organization so I became Silvirius, the first dark unicorn. And let me let you in on a little secret." He was standing right in front of the bars now. I seized my chance and struck. He seemed to notice that something was wrong at the last second and ducked to the left only to find a knife in his chest. I drove my knife in with so much force he toppled backward. Then he melted into a puddle of darkness.

"Let us go," the centaur said. "I have killed all the prison guards with my potion but more are coming if the alarm is sounded and I'd guess that the alarm is already sounded. So we must go," he concluded. "Climb on my back," he said. It was hard work getting on his back because of the two swords he carried and the bow and arrows. When we turned the first corner was when trouble hit. The centaur shot a demon between the eyes. But the real trouble came at the door. There were waves after waves of wraiths. "Close your eyes," the centaur ordered. Then the centaur muttered something under his breath and there was a light that almost blinded me even through my closed eyes."You can look now," she said. I looked and saw that the entire first three rows were now puddles. And the wraiths behind them were apparently blind because they started milling around, occasionally hacking at each other with their rapiers. "Now's our chance to escape," the centaur whispered. The blindness is only momentary, they will recover in minutes if not seconds so hold on." But I really did not get what "hold on" meant because at that moment he thundered off. At the same moment, everything else was in slow motion besides us and then suddenly a falcon was screeching overhead. I didn't know where it came from but it was there nonetheless. Sometime later I fell asleep which was surprising since the falcon was screeching so loudly. I had a dream where I was in a place that served steak and mashed potatoes and the soup! The pasta soup was heavenly even better than my mother's homemade recipe. Every spoonful of the soup reminded me of the sun. The mashed potatoes were so smooth that they could slide down my gullet. The steak was medium-rare, my favorite, and every bite reminded me of the steak my mom made but it was one hundred and one times better. And there was also iced tea and every sip of it felt refreshing like a cold, winter morning with the sun shining merrily and my mom and I throwing snowballs at each other. I ate and drank until I could eat no more. I felt as if my stomach was about to combust. But then in came the tiramisu. It was better than anything I had ever tasted. The rich smell of coffee wafted up from it. It reminded me of the coffee shop my mom went to when I was little. Despite the fact that my stomach was about to explode I managed to fit in three more slices of tiramisu before I could eat no more. But then came the Ice cream. It was my favorite flavor, mango. The ice cream was silky and sweet. It was like I was on a sunny June morning, a ray of sunlight shining in my face. The sensation intensified as mango juice dribbled down my chin like sunlight itself. I managed six scoops before I was sure my belly would explode. Every moment of eating the ice cream was sunsational. Finally came the float. It was vanilla ice cream on top of some Fanta even though my mom insisted root beer was one hundred times better. It tasted amazing. It was like the early spring making our ice crack in the pond on which my mother and I go ice skating every winter. It was happy but also sad at the same time as if my old life called back for me.

Screeeeeeech! A cry tore the morning in two. I sat up groggily only to find the centaur shooting at a falcon--the same one that I saw last night.

"Kill it," I ordered.

Then it seemed to fly further away than ever.

"What's wrong?" the centaur asked.

"That bird," I said. "I saw it last night."

"Oh, you did? When did you see it?"

"I saw it last night as we were escaping from the wraiths. Do you think it's a spy from Naquinn?" I asked.

"It has to be a spy for Naquinn."

"That's reassuring. But what do we do?"

"We tell Arfaa to prepare for war."

"Who's Arfaa?"

"My boss and the leader of the Blinding Light Organization."

"Yeah, about the Blinding Light Organization: what do you guys do?"

"We try to eliminate all evil." The conversation ended there and we lapsed into a friendly silence. I thought of asking him about a lot of other things but I was too tired and he said we still had four more hours to go.

I still had forgotten to ask his name so I asked, "What's your name?"

"I cannot tell you my true name but do you want to hear the name I go by?"

"Why can you not go by your true name?"

"Because if I told you my true name you would have a certain amount of power over me. Long ago a wicked king named Remuluos cursed us because we offended him. Our leader called him a dimwit and said that no human can match the wisdom of the centaurs. The king got very angry so he hunted down our ruler and tortured him to death. We managed to slay one thousand of his men before he got to our king. But alas! He got to our king and ordered his witch to curse us. The curse was not a simple one. For example, if you knew my true name you could convince me to do almost anything. She died in the process because the life energy that it took her to do the spell was immense. So do you want to hear the name I go by?"

"Yes, I do."

"My name is Frank." And with that, I drifted away into the comforts of sleep. Or discomforts of sleep.

4. Two Friends

Fire. Smoke. Screaming. Someone pounding on the door. A dark figure shrouded in shadow standing on a distant cliff. More fire, and more smoke. Then a woman came into the room and took my little body out the door and then we ran into a forest, heading toward the lights. The night air was damp as it pressed onto the person's back. It was a dark night thirteen years ago, only a sliver of a waning crescent moon setting in the west. When we were going towards the town I saw an impenetrable blackness that was swallowing up everything in its path. So I said the first word in my life, "no," but the person kept going. "No." I struggled even more.

Suddenly I woke up, gasping for air. Frank noticed my discomfort and asked, "What's wrong?" he asked.

"Nothing," I lied. Then a realization hit me. I was the boy in all the nightmares I'd been having. But how could I be? My mom was still alive. Then I thought about it a little more and wondered if I was fostered.

That's when Frank said, "Here we are." I had been so busy thinking about my past that I forgot the present. Before us stood a magnificent castle carved out of marble. It was not like a house that had a roof. There was a triangular wall surrounding something. It was huge! It was so big that a small town could fit in it. "Here we are, standing beside the greatest castle of all time, Eldresdore, named after the original Eldresdore," Frank said. "Let me introduce you to Arfaa." When he went up to the door he whispered something that was inaudible and the doors swung open to reveal a gentle golden light that bathed the room in puddles of gold only for me to realize that the puddles were real pools of liquid gold they were bubbling. Then a dragon stepped into view.

The dragon was not like you would imagine but a dragon nevertheless. I could tell from a first glance that Arfaa was male. He was magnificent! On his head, he wore a huge golden crown. He was easily five times as big as me. His wings were huge, easily as big as a jet. The way he held his chin high reminded me of the way a cobra looks when it is about to strike. He radiated warmth. He smelled like charcoal. Frank bowed before Arfaa and so did I.

That's when he spoke in a deep, resonant voice and I couldn't tell if it was through my mind or if it was through his mouth. Probably both. "Rise, Magus," he said, so I stood before him. Never have I felt so small and so weak or so dominated. That's when he spoke again. "I see that you realize that you are someone special. You are the nephew of the moon. You have a very strong magical ability. You were born to oppose Naquinn, the son of darkness."

"I'm supposed to fight against that creep and win?" I said thinking back to my dream.

"Yes, but I do not expect you to win yet. I will first show you to your cousin Andromeda. And remember, you are all family here. With a push comes a shove. Except for the unicorns and sprites, nymphs, elves, and fauns, the people here are all family. I will show you around the place before you see your cousin. Try to make some friends. And oh, Frank--come with us." As we walked down the halls of the castle we saw wondrous sights. On a hill, there was a miniature castle that was lined with red. On the opposite hill, there was another castle where there was a miniature castle lined with blue. There was also another hill that had an Olympic-sized swimming pool. A boy walked over to us. He was about seventeen. Frank waved at him. "Hi, Luke," he said.

"Hi, Frank. I see that your mission went well. And who might that be?"

"I'm Magus," I said.

"Luke."

"Hi, Luke," I said.

A boy came up and whispered something in Arfaa's ear. The dragon's face suddenly grew sterner and he said,

"Come with me, Frank and you, Luke, show Magus where Andromeda is."

"Okay," Luke said, then he began leading me toward another log cabin.

Then he said conversationally, "Your cousin

is very nice."

"I hope she is."

"Oh, here comes my sister," he said unenthusiastically, his smile dropping. Coming toward us was the most beautiful girl I'd ever seen his smile dropped even more.

"What's wrong?" I asked.

"It's just that Cassiopeia is the most annoying sister in the world."

"I'm not annoying."

"Yes, you are, little sister."

"Alright, alright, no more fighting." I didn't want to see my newly made friends fighting with each other. "Show me where my cousin lives."

But they were still fighting too hard to notice so I let out a string of curses under my breath and started toward the hut only to bump into an emerald wall of scales.

Watch your language, came the reply of an impossibly rich voice inside my head. I looked up at the wall only to find that it wasn't a wall but a real dragon almost as grand as Arfaa himself. This one was female and she looked like a snake about to strike with those heartless black eyes. She radiated danger. She smelled like burning flesh. She was much more dangerous than Arfaa ever was and would ever be. *My name is Cavia and I am the queen of this place.* Even Luke and Cassiopeia had stopped fighting to listen to Cavia speak. *First of all, watch your language, Magus and you and you,* she lifted one claw and pointed at Cassiopeia and Luke, *stop fighting or else one week of scrubbing toilets. Got it?* They both nodded. *I have urgent matters to attend. However, if I catch you fighting again…* She let the threat hang in the air and was off again with a whoosh of her wings. Immediately Luke said, "I will show you where your cousin lives." half out of fear.

"Who is his cousin?"

"Andromeda."

"Her? What a treat."

"You both know my cousin?"

"Yes, of course, we know her, she and I are the greatest strategists the Blinding Light has to offer. Though she is super annoying."

"You girls and your strategies, we boys like

to fight. And she's not annoying," Luke said. Just as we were almost at the cabin we veered right. I saw a small hole in the ground and Luke clambered into it. "Finally," I heard Cassiopeia say. I asked, "Does my cousin live down there?"

"Anyone with half of a brain wouldn't live there except for dwarves," she said.

"Then where does she live?"

"This is the secret passage that only Luke and Andromeda know about."

"Why them and not you?"

"Because they obviously think that I'm not important enough. Because I'm too small or something, but come on. I'm not small or young and your cousin's super bossy and my brother's super mean."

"Well, your brother said that she's super nice."

"She is to him and she respects Arfaa and Cavia and adores her hilliu that's made of pure light that was awarded to her when she got the record for slaying trolls. She slew eleven trolls in under thirty minutes. The only time she and I do get along is when we plan Capture the Castle..."

"Whoa! Whoa! Whoa! Slow down. First of all, Frank mentioned this being a hilliu." I pulled out my pocket knife and she examined it. Then her face contorted in rage.

"You killed Hope!" she screamed and with that, she thrust her pocket knife at me. I barely managed to deflect her pocket knife when a voice drifted up from the tunnel and asked,

"Hey, what's the commotion up there?"

"What's happening is that your sister is trying to kill me," I said, crossing blades with her, and then suddenly as if by magic she flew over me and almost stabbed me in the back with her sword... Almost. I was just quick enough to evade her blow. But how did the shiny gold knife transform into a sword? Then I realized. The hilliu could transform into other weapons. So I looked at it and imagined that it was a sword and surprisingly it obeyed but then I felt it being jerked out of my hand and now it was lying on the ground and Cassiopeia had her spear pointed at my belly and slowly and deliberately ground out the words,

"You killed Hope."

"I did not kill Hope. She is my mother. And she gave me this knife, " I said.

"I do not keep track of the outside world but I doubt that Hope had any children." We were interrupted by Luke and his noisy entrance. His forehead was sweaty and his breaths came in ragged gasps. He immediately saw Cassiopeia's spear and knocked it away with his sword.

"What are you doing?" she asked. "Can't you see that he is a threat? Don't you recognize Hope's hilliu?"

"I'd recognize it any day of the week," Luke said, "but the boy may not be lying. He may be telling the truth. Arfaa trusted him. Take him to Andromeda immediately. We need to know if he is safe from a more reliable source."

They escorted me down the corridor with their spears poking uncomfortably against my back and just as I thought that the heat was getting unbearable we went up up and up. The walk took about fifteen minutes. Then suddenly the floor dropped from underneath us and we tumbled down a few feet and dropped on a soft mattress. Luke was laughing and Cassiopeia was so surprised that she almost stabbed me with her hilliu. Then I noticed someone standing in front of us: a girl with silver hair who lifted her bow and aimed it at me straight for the heart, my heart, and released the arrow.

5. The Son of the Sun

The arrow whizzed towards my heart. One second it was moving at a normal rate the next moment it was like the arrow was in slow motion but it was still fast. My hand was in front of me so I caught it, flipped it over, leaped from my spot in the bed and held it up to the silver-haired girl's chin and asked,

"What's the big idea?" But she was just as fast and did a somersault and landed behind me. I was done playing games. I spun around and thanks to all the training of my mother's I managed to deliver a kick powerful enough to send the girl sprawling against the wall, winded. She was almost fast enough to recover but I pounced and slammed her against the wall, used an elbow to lock her chest against the wall and pressed the arrow against her neck hard enough to draw blood and tell her that if she resisted she would be a dead girl. She gulped. Then I asked again, "What's the big idea?" I could hear footsteps coming. I turned my head around to see Luke and Cassiopeia advancing on me. Just last year my mom had said never to show any opponent any mercy in any fight. She had told me to write and repeat sixty times. After all those hours drilling it into my head, I remembered now so I said, "Come one step closer and I will put the arrow through her." The girl gulped again. "My mom told me never to show any mercy in a fight," I said.

"That sounds like something Hope would say. I believe you," Cassiopeia stated.

"And I, too," Luke said.

"And I," the girl croaked. I let the arrow withdraw a little so she could breathe

"How do you know what happened in the tunnels?"

"I can read minds," she said.

"Then why did you shoot me with that arrow?"

"It was a test to see if you were worthy enough to join the organization."

"What if I had died?"

"Then we would know that you are not a

child of nature."

"But then what if the person isn't a child of nature…?"

"Then they die," she shrugged. "Mortals aren't as important as we are, obviously. A great human leader proved that. His name was Dwight D. Eisenhower. We offered him a bargain during World War Two. It went like this: We helped him with his war and he helped us with ours. We offered the same bargain to Hitler first since he was obviously the more powerful of the two but after a warm welcome, one of his top generals murdered the ambassador. Just as we were about to ask Hitler again one of our spies in America caught a whiff of something. He said that it was going to be the biggest sea invasion in history and that the Americans seemed very confident about winning. So we asked them if they would accept the deal and they said yes so we planned the invasion. He used his mortal soldiers on the ground while we watched from a safe distance. The weapons that the French resistance did not destroy we did with our powers so he sacrificed many men to win the war and that is what we must do to win this war. Each one of us has a power that is unique to us, passed down by our parents... For me, it is this." She shot two beams of silver energy from her hands at a target that had ten arrows sticking out of the bull's eye.

"Wow," I whispered. Then Cassiopeia and Luke jumped and looked like they were surfing on air, they were literally flying. Then they jumped back down. "Double wow! But you said that you got those powers from your godly parents. So then, who is my godly parent?"

"First of all our parents aren't godly, just natural--like wind, air, and even war," said the girl.

"How is war natural?"

"War is the natural cycle of things just like when there are times of few and times of plenty. There are times of war and times of peace. And also I think you know who your father is."

"Please, I don't know."

"Yes, you do."

"I don't know who my father is. Please just be straightforward about it," I begged.

"You know who he is."

"Please just tell me, I don't know who my father is." I paused for a moment. "Wait! it can't be!"

A slow smile crept across the girl's face.

"You know," she said.

"P-please, I don't know, that was just a wild assumption."

She snorted then said, "Isn't it obvious? You are the boy from your dreams. Arfaa hinted at it. But you were born to slay Naquinn. You are the son of the sun."

6. Naquinn's Impressive Army

"Impossible," chorused all the voices in the room except for mine and the girl's.

"Why?" I asked.

"Because absolutely no son of the sun has ever been born in two thousand years. There is a prophecy that says that a mighty hero, a son of the sun, will defeat Naquinn, Rhamal, and with the help of the sun eventually defeat Evile, the queen of darkness and evil. But the prophecy calls for a hero, not a young boy," Luke said.

"I'm not a young boy," I shouted.

"You are young compared to every one of us. Your grandmother is young, do you know how old we are?" asked Luke.

"Yes, you are about eighteen she is about sixteen and the other girl is about seventeen."

"Yes, we do look seventeen, eighteen, and sixteen. But in mortal years we are about thirteen centuries-old and she," he pointed at the other girl, "is about two-millennia old."

"Impossible."

"Naquinn, unlike us, is about two-eons old," Luke said.

"Impossible!" I exclaimed.

"It's true," he said. "Evile is the queen of darkness. She was born at the beginning of time," Luke said.

"Even more impossible. If you want to tell lies at least tell more believable ones. No one lives thirteen centuries or two millennia much less two eons old." I said.

"It is possible," Luke said.

"Listen," I said. They all stopped the conversation. "Do you hear that?" I asked. I heard trumpets blaring three notes before they stopped and blared the same three notes again. Over and over and over and over and over again. They all stared wide-eyed at each other.

"Is it possible?" I heard Cassiopeia say.

"Yep, we are under attack, all because of him," she pointed at me, "and that stupid, blundering, dimwitted centaur," the girl shouted. Who did this girl think she was? I was just about to say something when Luke said, "How dare you speak of Frank that way! Who do you think you are? You think you are better than every one of us here just because you are the daughter of the moon. You think that the moon is better than the wind. Well, guess what, it isn't!" Luke shouted, his face red with rage. "Frank is a really good friend."

"I'm sorry," the girl said genuinely. She must have really respected Luke or something because before that she looked about ready to explode. "We have to go to the castle now," Cassiopeia said seriously.

Fifteen minutes later we were at the castle. Arfaa rushed up to us and said, "Glad you guys came. I need to speak alone with Magus." The others left and that left me alone with Arfaa. "I need to give you something," he said. He opened his hand to reveal a glowing knife. "This is a hilliu made from pure light. You may find it useful during a fight. I understand that Hope trained you," he said.

"Yes."

"Fight well Magus. Use hate, but do not let it blind you." With that, he spread his massive red wings and spiraled off into the blue cloudless sky.

I looked at the knife given to me. It was made of pure light, I could easily tell. It was flawless and thrummed under my touch.

"Thank you," I whispered. The knife began humming.

Three deafening blasts tore through the castle.

"Follow me," Cassiopeia said and dragged me after her. It was as if she had appeared out of thin air. I stumbled and managed to regain my footing. At the top of the castle walls, I saw a sight that sent a shiver down my spine. On the horizon was a giant army of bees. But as I looked closer they weren't bees but wraiths. Waves upon waves of wraiths. Behind them came twelve-foot tall demons and giants. The giants were twenty-four-foot tall brutes with thick, muscular arms and legs and were holding clubs that could easily swipe away five men with one swing. And finally in the center of the army rode Naquinn--or at least I thought it was Naquin--on a chariot drawn by witches on their broomsticks and wolves.

On our side, we had some people in armor riding on their pegasus. We had centaur archers positioned on one of our towers we had some catapults, some men and women with pointed ears that I assumed were elves, we also had some unicorns, good ones, not like Alex. the unicorns were pearly white. Others were in human form like Alex when he first lured me into trusting him. I could tell that they were unicorns because they held their long horns like swords. We also had two dragons circling overhead.

"Stop gaping and come on!" Cassiopeia whispered fiercely in my ear. Making me jump.

"Why don't you guys use cannons or guns?" I asked.

"Because everything malfunctions here."

"What about those catapults?"

"Fine, only the simplest machines work here in Eldresdore. because the magic causes them to malfunction. "

"We're in eldest-what?"

"Rumor has it that Eldresdore is the ruins of a castle that lies in the west on an island in the black sea, past the Lost Lands. The whole land was named after the first castle," she said. We lapsed into a friendly sort of silence until we got to the catapults. They were huge close-up, even bigger than they had seemed on the parapet. Stocked up by them were ceramic balls.

"What are those ceramic balls for?" I asked.

"They are for the catapults," she said in a mother-explaining-something-to-a-young-child type of voice.

"I know that they are for the catapults," I said, "but why ceramic globes?"

"Because Arfaa has some nasty surprises inside of them for our dark foes. We are defending the castle keep," Cassiopeia said, "but first we need to get you a pegasus. Every pegasus chooses its rider, you know. If a pegasus doesn't like you and you try to ride it the pegasus will trample you."

"Wow, so I'm riding a flying horse into battle?"

"Yes, have you ever trained with Hope on a horse?"

"Yes, I have."

"Good, Hope taught you a lot."

"Yes, she did. I was wondering why she always trained me instead of letting me play video games."

"This is the stable," she said, "it has all the horses and pegasuses." We entered the stable, and my mind was immediately drawn toward the white horse that was in the center. I moved towards it. "No!" Cassiopeia said and tried to grab me but I wrenched away from her grasp. The pegasus in front of me was the most beautiful thing I had ever laid my eyes upon. I felt an urge to touch it and so I did.

A blinding flash, then darkness. It took a full minute for my eyes to adjust. After I could see again the pegasus leaned down and nuzzled its muzzle against my cheek. Its breath was warm. I sensed another consciousness brushing against my thoughts. It was like Arfaa's but warmer and more gentle and even older. *Hello, little one*, came a deep and ancient voice.

"Wow," Cassiopeia breathed, "do you know what you have done?"

"No, I do not know what I have done. So am I this pegasus's rider?"

"First of all, you are his rider. Second of all, he has never let a person this close to him without causing severe wounds. And most importantly, he isn't just a pegasus but Pegasus, the immortal lord of horses. A prophecy once said that whoever harnesses Pegasus will be immortal."

"So I'm immortal?" *Yes, little one, you are, but you can still die from wounds*, came the whisper from the Pegasus. I did not mind the pegasus calling me little one. On the contrary, I kind of liked it. *Naquin's army is on the move*, came the voice of the pegasus. *Climb onto my back and I will carry you to the keep*

"How will you come?" I asked Cassiopeia.

"I will fly," came the curt reply. Oh right! I forgot that she could fly.

We flew towards the keep.

"Do you have a pegasus?"

"I do, and his name is Treinin. He is waiting for us at the keep. The tower is invincible," she said, "but if our enemies take it then they will have a major stepping stone toward Etresid, the home of the elves, and if they overwhelm us the elves won't stand a chance. Then they will take Ur-huem, the home of the dwarves, as easily as a frog catching a fly with its tongue. They will then build a ship and Naquinn and a few select werewolves and demons will sail with him on the black sea. March into the Lost Lands, and to the ruins of Eldresdore. An ancient evil lies there, an evil born at the beginning of time. If the evil is wakened it will annihilate everything in its path. Naquinn thinks that he can harness the power of the shadow."

"It's called the shadow?"

"Yes. Naquinn understands darkness but compared to the shadow he only knows it at a basic level. If he unleashes the shadow it will destroy everything. It will destroy the whole universe and suck on Naquinn, Rahmal, and Evile's darkness for the rest of eternity."

"How do you know about the shadow?" I asked.

"I know about the shadow because it is taught in class," she said.

"You take classes here? I thought you only trained here."

"We train most of the time but we learn about the history of Eldresdore and what weak spots are on a demon or other foul creature."

Trumpets blasted. "That's our signal," she said. She whistled and a pegasus that was black as night came and dove below Cassiopeia and swooped up. Suddenly there was a deafening crack as all the catapults released at once. "Follow me," she said. And I followed Cassiopeia to the walls of the castle. I saw scaling ladders brought by the monsters so I pulled out my hilliu and willed it to turn into a saw, waited until the monsters were three-quarters of the way up, and sawed my way through the ladder. It was hard work because the wood was obviously enchanted. I had to stay balanced on Pegasus while sawing away the wood. I saw monsters closing their distance. I brushed his consciousness and said, *Kick those baddies off for me, will you?*

Of course. The first demon smashed into us but Pegasus kicked him off the ladder. The second one came and Pegasus toppled him backward and like in dominoes he toppled backward onto the unsuspecting demon behind him and he toppled backward and so on and so on. Then, when all of them had stopped playing dominoes, with all my strength I heaved the ladder free and crashed it on top of the demons. *Thank you, but I have to do this on my own. Keep bashing demon heads and you will do just fine.*

You are welcome, he said and let me down on the wall. I charged into the fray, stabbing, slashing, and gutting all the monsters that I saw. My hilliu was a deadly arc of destruction. Suddenly a giant's club bashed the wall. It sent shrapnel flying everywhere and a piece, a small piece, flew into my arm and lodged there. It hurt but it was not a serious wound. Once I fell off my bike and it hurt more than this. I ran to a hiding spot, soaked the wound in water with my water bottle, and plucked it out. It hurt more than anything now but since my mom had taught me how to do this I dumped water on it again, cut off part of my shirt with my hilliu and bound it tightly to my arm, and just had enough time to spare to kill a wraith who was trying to stab me with its knife. After I got bandaged up, I hid there and rested for a few more minutes. Then I leaped from my hiding spot, killed a wolf, jumped onto the wall, leaped from the wall onto a giant's back, slid down the length of it with my hilliu as a sword, jumped down, and landed running. I slashed left and right, stabbed back and forth, and every slash and stab claimed the life of at least one monster. I slashed and stabbed until I got tired and rested. There were too many of them, I thought despairingly. Then I caught sight of Naquinn fighting on the battlements and a thought crossed my mind. *Pegasus?*

Yes? I know that you're planning something, I can feel it. The fight is not going well up here either. The ravens are killing us one by one. They have poison in their claws. We are usually immune to poison but this is unlike any poison I have ever heard of. So once again, do you have a plan?

Of course, I do, We are going to cut the head off that snake.

7.   The Big Bam

I know what you are going to say and no, you can't, it's too dangerous. The risk is not ours to take. But it is my destiny so why not now?

I was not going to say that. I was going to agree with you. Even though I don't like it I still think that it is necessary in order for us to win this battle. Just wait for me. It might take a couple of minutes for me to get down there so get prepared for your battle with Naquinn. Besides, you might not win this battle because it said a son of the sun will be able to defeat Naquinn it doesn't mean that you will be the one to defeat Naquinn.

Gee, thanks for the encouragement.

I did not mean that. What I meant is that you have to be careful.

I know.

The next thing I knew I was swooped up from the ground and riding on the back of Pegasus. The Pegasus. Never in my life have I ever felt prouder.

So? How do I challenge him?

Say this: Naquinn! I challenge you in single combat!

I saw Naquinn pouring dark energy from his palms at the girl with the silver hair and I saw the girl meet it with a silverish energy from her own palms. Arfaa was in the sky with Cavia, one blowing fire and the other spitting acid on Naquinn. I could tell it was acid because it melted everything but Naquinn. The fire and the acid couldn't melt Naquinn so Arfaa tried diving at Naquinn but Naquinn muttered something and Arfaa was forced to retreat.

Then I yelled, "Naquinn! I challenge you in single combat!"

"I ACCEPT!" he yelled.

"No!" Arfaa roared, "You weren't ready! But remember my advice: Use anger, but do not let it blind you."

So Naquinn and I squared off. People and monsters stood in a ring around us. Naquinn sent a bolt of dark energy flying at my shoulder. I barely managed to jump aside with a yelp. He laughed.

That was the last straw for me. I hated him. I hated the way he laughed. I hated his darkness. So I did the natural thing: I charged at him. And he charged at me. A scream tore from my lips. At that same moment, a yellow sort of laser shot from my hilliu, but Naquinn met it with dark energy of his own. This sudden exchange of energy jolted us both in different directions. I charged at him again. This time there was no magic from either of us. I met his sword just as he swung at me. He stood there, each of us trying to push each other over. I willed my sword to morph into a spear to catch Naquinn off guard then follow up with a stab, but no such luck. He produced a hunting knife from his robes and slashed my spear out of the deadlock. Then, just taking a moment to balance it, he threw the knife spinning toward my throat. I barely managed to catch it. I threw it at him. He caught it, threw it back at me.

"Hot potato one, hot potato two, hot potato three," he said and smiled evilly. I threw the knife back at him and said in turn.

"Hot potato one, hot potato two…," the knife

was sent spinning toward me. A deadly game of hot potato in a ring. Eventually, he got tired of this game and threw the knife at Luke, who was watching in the front row. I gasped. But Luke caught the knife and gave it to Arfaa. I was so distracted by the crowd that I didn't see Naquinn charging at me until the last second. I barely managed to deflect the thrust. I ran to the other side of the circle.

"Scared?" he taunted. "Babies are scared. You don't look like a baby to me. Unless you're a big fat baby. Are you a big fat baby?" I quickly got tired of his taunting. So I dropped my sword, screamed, and unleashed a torrent of my energy at him. He met it with his own dark energy. I could feel myself getting weaker every second. But I managed to keep up for a few more minutes. I was so tired and so desperate to not die that my magic ate away his dark energy. Just as I thought I was about to win the battle, he used his sword to eat up my energy. I picked up my sword and charged at him again. We clashed. Sparks flew. I hacked at him over and over again. We tried to break into each other's defenses. I shot a bolt of energy from my hilliu but he deflected it with his own dark energy. Once again I swiped at him, he swiped at me, and we locked blades, each of us trying to push the other over. Our swords hissed and scraped. I tried the same maneuver. I willed my hilliu to become a spear. It became a spear... and it skewered Naquinn in the gut. He melted into a puddle before I had the chance to stab him again.

"Behind you!" Luke shouted.

"Curse you, boy," Naquinn shouted from behind me. He drew a throwing knife and sent it spinning toward Luke. With a flick of Luke's wrist, the knife stopped and was sent spinning back to Naquinn. It landed on the ground at his feet.

"Why aren't you dead? I thought that I stabbed you."

"You certainly did. But for your information, I am invincible." My heart sank. How am I supposed to defeat someone who's invincible?

"He's lying," Cassiopeia shouted, "you can kill him through a stab in the heart or with your energy."

"You interfering little brat!" Naquinn yelled. He sent knife after knife after knife toward Cassiopeia's chest. She caught one after another after another but the last one Naguinn sent at her arm she failed to catch. The blade embedded itself deep in her arm. And Arfaa told someone else to carry the body away.

"NO!" I screamed. I charged Naquinn again and he charged me. I struck at his heart once, twice, three times, four times, five times, six times, seven times. None of the thrusts seemed to go through to the heart.

"I told you that I am invincible. Trying to stab through my amandant breastplate is like trying to shoot through one of your human quarters with one of your human airguns. Only my sword can stab through it."

"There is a way to defeat him!" Luke shouted. "You can use your energy to kill him. If your energy touches even one part of him, he dies."

"No!" Naquinn cried. "You revealed my secret and so you will die for it." He shot bolt after bolt of dark energy toward Luke. I was growing quite fond of Luke and Cassiopeia because one told me how to stab Naquinn and the other told me about his fatal weakness so I deflected the dark energy into the sky so that Luke didn't get hit by it. And then I charged at Naquinn. This time he did not charge me. Instead, he stood there waiting for the attack to come. So I did something unexpected. I dropped my weapon and used my energy against Naquinn. He deflected my energy with his own special dark energy. I soon wore him out and forced him to suck my light into his sword. I was already so exhausted that if he allowed me to sleep then I might have never woken up. But I didn't care. *What could I lose if I died?* I thought. *I could lose my pegasus, my mom, and my life.* But I didn't care anymore. Reason told me to stop. But anger told me not to. Anger won. I channeled all my anger and used it as strength. Naquin's blade began to glow. I summoned more of my hatred for him. Probably the anger and only the anger could have fueled me to keep going. I kept going. It was tiring out. I knew it, but I did not care. It felt like carrying a car while swimming but I was determined to do it. *Everything depends on me*, I thought. If I died everyone else would die and that gave me the courage to keep going. *If I'm going to die*, I thought, *I might as well die fighting*. The sword was shining like a star now. Naquinn was trying to charge at me but my energy was holding his sword back and he had no way to charge me without a sword. The sword was shining brighter than the sun now. And any moment it might explode. That was my plan. Once the sword had started to shine I had solidified the plan. I knew it might kill me. The sword was vibrating so much now that I knew it was going to explode. It was shining so brightly that I had to avert my eyes.

"Duck," I tried to yell but it came out more like a croak. At least everyone heard me so they formed a giant turtle formation. The giant turtle formation-- my mom had taught me this. The giant turtle formation is when shields overlap forming a giant wall, sort of like a turtle shell. I knew the sword was going to blow soon so I crawled into my own shield while still shooting beams of light. It was hard work. But I managed to do it just in time. The sword exploded with a big bang and a burst of blinding light sent shrapnel flying everywhere. Then all went black.

8. The Blessing

I was gasping for air. Every breath I took was painful. The air seemed to scorch my throat. It was like drinking lava and acid at the same time.

"Wake up!" someone called. "Wake up! Wake up! Wake up! Wake up!"

"Go away," I mumbled, still half asleep.

The voice came again. "Wake up! Wake up! Wake up! Wake up!" The voice sounded more urgent this time. "Wake up or you will die!" came the voice again.

"I said go away. Go away. Go away. Go away. Go away! Go away! Go away!" I was practically shouting at the end. I jolted awake and saw that I was in a bed with white sheets. Arfaa, Cavia, Luke, Cassiopeia, and Pegasus were all looming over me.

"We thought you weren't going to make it," Cassiopeia explained.

"What were you thinking?" Luke asked.

"You could have died using all that energy. What would we have done if you had died? We would have died if you died."

"I, at that moment, actually didn't care if I died."

"You what?"

Are you all right little one? Came the tentative whisper of Pegasus's mind.

I am all right. I reached up to touch Pegasus's muzzle and he ducked his head down to sniff me.

I could feel your life force draining away from you, Pegasus said. *Let us take a moment to celebrate the fact that you are still here with us and have not yet drifted away into the realm of death. If you had died I would have been closer to death then I ever was. Loneliness is a kind of death too, you know. I would have lost the will to live if you had died.*

You can't die though, I thought you were immortal.

As I said, loneliness is a kind of death too. So as I said, let us take a moment to celebrate the fact that you are still here with us and have not yet drifted away into the realm of death. We were silent for a moment, our hearts beating in rhythm. Arfaa, Cavia, and Luke left. The only ones remaining were Cassiopeia, Pegasus, and me. I stared into pegasus's deep amber eyes and patted his head.

"Good boy," I said. I felt my connection with Pegasus deepen. Pegasus whinnied softly.

Then I asked Cassiopeia coldly, "why are you here?"

"Because I have a blessing for you," she said.

"What blessing?" I asked, instantly suspicious.

"The gift of the winds, of course," she said. "Since my mother is the goddess of the winds I can give anyone, but only one person, the power of controlling the winds, and I saw how bravely you fought three days ago."

"Wait, I was out for three days?"

"Yes, you were out for three days. Anyway, it might help in the coming battle."

"Another battle?"

"Yes, another battle. You were out for three days. After you killed Naquinn."

"Wait, I killed Naquinn?"

"Yes, of course, you killed Naquinn. A piece of his sword embedded itself in his heart. Anyway, after that, the monsters fled. We killed most of them after they dispersed. Unfortunately, they have gathered reinforcements and twenty thousand of Naquinn's troops are headed this way."

"That sucks. But won't they give up after Naquinn dies?"

"I know. Anyway, as I was saying, my brother gave the gift of the winds to Andromeda."

"Wait, who's Andromeda?"

"She's your cousin. Anyway..."

"Wait, I thought you and Luke were going to lead me to my cousin. Instead, you guys led me to a complaining silver-haired girl."

"That complaining silver-haired girl as you put it is your cousin. Anyway..."

"She can't be. Luke said that my cousin is nice. And the complaining silver-haired girl is so mean that I was tempted to snap her nose off."

"You wouldn't have gotten very far with that," she laughed.

"What makes you think that?"

"She's had two millennia of practice time…"

"Well, Naquinn had two eons of practice time."

"Point taken. But you were destined to kill Naquinn."

"Excuses, excuses, and more excuses," I muttered. "But I might not have been the one to kill him. The prophecy, as Pegasus puts it, says that a son of the sun will eventually defeat Naquinn. The prophecy never specifies which son of the sun will eventually kill him."

"I get it! You're saying that better than Andromeda."

"I am better than Andromeda in some ways. For example, I don't insult centaurs for no apparent reason."

"I agree that with you that she is mean."

"You do?"

"Yes I do, but will you please stop interrupting me?"

"Fine."

"That was an interruption, have I made myself clear?"

I nodded.

"Okay, great, so what I was saying was that Luke gave his power to Andromeda and that I am going to give mine to you."

"Thank you," I said, "but why can't I give my power to another person?"

"Because you are not a twin," she said.

"Could've fooled me. You look much younger than him."

"I look much younger and am much smaller because I've spent less time in the mortal world than him."

"You mean--?"

"Yes, time stops here in Eldresdore. Well… not completely. One month in the mortal world is like one thousand years here. Anyway, do you accept my gift?"

"I do."

"This might take a few minutes," she said.

Then she put a hand on my forehead and

started chanting. The chanting increased in volume every minute. As the chanting increased in volume and speed she began to glow. Brighter and brighter the chanting crescendoed and accelerated until she started to glow like a miniature sun. The chanting rose louder, faster, and she glowed brighter. I could feel the palm of her hand uncomfortably warm against my forehead. The chanting was deafening now and the light was blinding. I could feel her hand transferring energy into me. The energy that I wanted. I could feel myself getting stronger by the second. I felt a breeze settle over me. When I opened my eyes not only could I feel the breeze I could also see it. My perception of the wind was getting stronger by the second. She glowed even brighter. Then she stopped glowing. She slumped against the bed. I could literally see steam rising from her skin.

"Medic!" I shouted "Medic! Medic! Medic! I need a medic! I need a doctor!"

"It's all right," came a voice from the corner and Luke emerged, stepping out of the door.

"How did you appear?" I asked.

"I was making sure that my sister was going to be okay because I know what happens when you expend too much energy in a small amount of time. She'll be fine in about an hour or two," he said.

"What was that chanting all about?"

"Chanting is the only way to transfer energy from yourself to another person safely. If you don't chant you can die and the other person might explode."

"Wow. Harsh."

"I agree, but you know what's harsher?"

"What?"

"What you said about Andromeda. She's a very nice person. If you keep talking about her that way I'll have to not be friends with you anymore."

"You'll not be friends with me just because I hate her?"

"That's right. You got it straight. And if you keep saying that you hate her I'll have to not talk to you."

"You'll do all that just because I hate her?"

"Yes. Also, get yourself rested. We need you in the battle."

"When is the battle?"

"Naquinn's army is moving fast."

"But I thought Naquinn is dead?"

"He is. But the rest of his army isn't."

"Phew. I thought for a second that Naquinn came back to the land of the living."

"Naquinn's army will be here by sundown tomorrow so you better get some rest."

"No, I'll get some rest once I've had food. I'm starving. And I'm thirsty."

"No doubt you are, you haven't had food in three days, or water for that matter. Dinner's in an hour but I bet there are some pastries in the kitchen and I doubt the chef would mind. After all, you killed Naquinn. What would you like?"

"Since it's before dinner I'll have a box of six donuts and a jug of iced tea."

"What type of donuts?"

"Umm... I want three of them jelly with chocolate frosting. And three of them with chocolate frosting. And make sure the iced tea is sweet and grab some sugar packets if you have any."

"Unhealthy, but all right," Luke said as he walked out the door.

A few minutes later Luke came in whistling and carrying two cups, a jug of iced tea, sugar packets and a box of donuts.

"Thanks, Luke."

"You're welcome," he said. He sat down on the chair opposite of mine next to the bed.

"Do I smell donuts?" came a moan from the bed.

"Cassiopeia, you're awake!" Luke said.

"I am. Once again, do you have donuts?" she asked hopefully.

"We do," I said, "we have plenty for everyone so come and join us for donuts and iced tea."

Luke pulled a chair from the wall.

"Thanks," Cassiopeia said.

"There is a problem," Luke said, "we have three people but only two cups."

"I'll use the jug," I said.

I poured iced tea into the cups until they were full.

"Enough?"

They both nodded. Cassiopeia was eyeing the donuts greedily. I gave one to her and one to Luke.

"Enough?"

They both nodded. Then I took the sugar packets, ripped them open and poured them in. I swirled the tea around and gulped it down. Then I dug in.

9.   The Best Dinner Ever

I dug my face into the donuts and devoured one after another. I finished two donuts in a matter of seconds. After that I gulped down three mouthfuls of the sweet tea, not caring if it sploshed on my shirt. The iced tea was delicious. It was even better than Fanta. Luke and Cassiopeia finished their donuts in a more, let's say, civilized fashion.

"What's this whole Naquinn's army thing about?" I asked as I stuffed another donut into my mouth.

"What this is all about is that a part of Naquinn's army is dead but most of his army is not. As I said, twenty thousand troops are headed this way as we speak. Arfaa and Cavia have set up an ingenious trap to kill some of them but unfortunately, there is a necromancer with them."

"What's a necromancer?" I asked. But I thought I already knew and I hoped against hope that I was wrong.

"Someone who can bring back the dead,"

Luke said

"So can he bring back Naquinn?" I asked with a sinking feeling in my gut.

"Fortunately he can't. He can't bring back anyone more powerful than he is to the land of the living," Cassiopeia said

"Phew, I thought for a second that we were fighting Naquinn again. But what makes a necromancer so powerful? Couldn't Arfaa just blowtorch him?" I asked through a mouth full of donuts. As the last one disappeared Cassiopeia said,

"That's the problem, you can't kill him that way. He can only be killed with an arrow that is not on fire. He'll just revive if you kill him any other way."

"So why can't Arfaa or Cavia just drop an arrow on the necromancer, whoever he is?"

"That would theoretically work, but a dragon can only aim from the mouth."

"Then use a dragon-sized blowgun," I said.

"That should work, but when dragons try to blow air they blow fire instead."

"Then use a metal blowgun."

"Dragon fire can melt most metals."

"Then use tungsten or something. Dragon fire is not above six thousand degrees Fahrenheit."

"Dragon fire is above five thousand seven hundred degrees Fahrenheit so it will work. We have plenty of forges. But the thing is the arrow."

"What about it?"

"You can't use a wood arrow. Because even if it doesn't just burn to ashes. An arrow caught on fire won't work. Also, dragon fire shoots as far as fifty meters."

"I know you can't but you can use a carbon arrow."

"What about the fletchings?"

"We can use a lightweight metal for the feathers."

"Okay. we'll do it. But first, get some rest before dinner."

"Okay. Okay. Okay," I said.

"Get some sleep now."

"Okay. Okay. Okay. Fine."

I went back to bed. I couldn't sleep. I kept

thinking back to the fight with Naquinn. If I had died everyone would have died. What if a piece of the blade struck me in the heart instead of Naquinn? What if I had died before the blade exploded? I kept thinking back to the fight again and again. I eventually got so tired that I fell asleep. It was the same dream again.

Naquinn gave a frustrated yell and drew another knife. It was nothing like what you would ever expect from a knife. It was a blade and it was so dark that if you gazed into it for more than three seconds it would start sucking the soul from you. It was a weapon of pure evil. Just as Naquinn thrust his knife down, a beam of blinding light swallowed it. Then a booming voice said, "Leave my son alone, the police will be here soon." Then Naquinn said whispered in a slithery voice, *We will deal with this later*, and he and the snake vanished into a pool of darkness.

Then the dream showed me glimpses of my journey here. The falcon, the blinding light, the fight with Cassiopeia, the test with Andromeda, the pegasus, and the battle. It was all disjointed and blurry. After that, it zoomed in on one crucial detail, my fight with Naquinn. It was like watching through a misty spyglass and when all the fog was cleared away was my fight with Naquinn. I could see myself making the challenge on my pegasus, me dropping to the ground, and Naquinn accepting it and the shock on everyone's faces. Me charging and the deadly game of hot potato. I saw the knife go spinning toward Luke, him catching it. Me stabbing Naquinn. Him reviving. And then eventually me giving off the energy, his sword exploding and sending him sprawling back ten feet right into a hole covered by bushes. Him melting and his armor sinking into the bushes. That's ironic, I thought. He almost killed me when I was a baby but now I had killed him.

"Magus. Magus," someone gently shook me awake. It was Cassiopeia. "Time for dinner," she said.

"I have two questions," I said. "First of all, why did I have to stab Naquinn in the heart? And second, did you find his body anywhere?"

"We did not find his body anywhere. And

also you have to stab Naquinn in the heart because he has no heart."

"What do you mean?"

"What I mean is that you have to stab him through the heart."

"I know. But you said that he had no heart."

"I know it's confusing but that's what you have to do. We can discuss more of this at dinner. Luke knows more about it than I do."

"Okay."

She led me out of the hospital and toward the dining hall. The dining hall was huge. The room was a rectangular prism. The ceiling was very high. The hall was easily four hundred feet long. There was a red carpet draped across one end of the hall with a gold dragon sewn on. People sat everywhere, chatting and arguing. She led me toward the table where Luke and Andromeda were sitting in a corner and plopped down. I sat down next to Luke.

"I have a question to have you answer," I said.

"What?" he asked.

"Why did…"

I was interrupted by Arfaa's booming voice. Everyone looked to the red carpet that was draped across the end of the hall. Standing beside Arfaa was Cavia. They both looked as grand as ever but a little worse for wear. But that just made them look fiercer. Arfaa had a deep gash on his neck that was dripping black ooze. He also had a narrow cut along his back that was almost healed. Cavia had had a stab that was probably made by an arrow. It was bandaged up and treated but I could see dried blood and the skin around it was turning purple. People started to murmur.

"SILENCE!" Arfaa roared. Murmuring stopped. Then he continued in a more reasonable tone. "We are lucky to be here this evening. We are lucky to be chatting with each other this evening. We are lucky that Magus is here with us."

He gestured at me. Heads turned to me in wonder.

"For those who do not know, Magus killed Naquinn."

This brought a round of applause and

cheering.

"And most of all, we are lucky that we have not wandered into the land of the dead. And a moment of silence for our friends who have."

We were all silent for a moment.

"Also we have a special guest. Many of you look up to her. She is called the bane of the basilisk. She is called Hope Cobra."

At this everybody clapped and cheered.

"I didn't know that my mom was this famous here."

"Your foster mom," Andromeda said coldly.

"Whatever."

"Just teasing," she said.

I watched as my mom headed towards us.

"Mom!"

"Magus!"

My mom came toward our table.

She hugged me and asked, "What were you thinking? Tell me everything once the trays are served."

"Okay, but in the meantime, I have some questions for you," I said.

"How are you guys holding up?" she asked Luke, Andromeda, and Cassiopeia.

"You know them?"

"Of course, I've known them since the eleventh century. I'm a daughter of Strategy."

"I have some questions, mom."

"Ask away, Magus, ask away."

"First of all, why did you not tell me about this place?"

"Because I thought it was too dangerous for you when you were twelve. I was too selfish. I couldn't let you go. So I trained you instead. Many people come here at the age of twelve."

"Why did I have to stab Naquinn through the heart?"

"Wait? You were the one that killed Naquinn?"

"Yes, mom, I was the one who killed Naquinn. Didn't Arfaa tell you? Again, why did I have to stab him through the heart?"

"No Arfaa didn't, probably because he wanted me to tell you or something. The answer is complicated but the simplest way to tell you is because he had a heart of ice."

"But Cassiopeia told me that he had no heart. And I thought that her answer was incomplete." I looked to Cassiopeia but she wasn't there and neither was Luke or Andromeda.

"Where did they go?"

"They went to get food. Anyway, Cassiopeia in a way is correct because a heart of ice is almost like having no heart. Also, once you stab him his heart freezes and he will die."

"How does he do that?"

"Do what?"

"Not die by me stabbing him through the stomach."

"I don't know."

"Fine, I'm getting some food. If you can find an answer tell me."

"Okay."

I went to the back of the line where Luke, Cassiopeia, and Andromeda were waiting. I noticed one odd fact. There was no food. There were only humongous trays and glasses served. What had my mom said, When the trays were served?

"Where's the food?" I asked.

"If you would only look, you would see," Andromeda said. This brought laughter from all of them. I was liking her less and less. Cassiopeia probably pitied me so she said, "The food comes from the trays."

"What do you mean?"

"What I mean is that the food comes from the trays."

"How?"

"Okay, so first you say what you want for the main course."

"What do you mean?"

"Just what I meant."

"Umm, okay I want, hmm, a twelve-ounce steak medium rare on a bagel with mac and cheese and cauliflower."

"Okay, next say what you want for soup."

"Chicken noodle soup."

"Next, what do you want for dessert?"

"Fanta float."

"That is a job for the glasses. What do you want to drink? Anything non-alcoholic of course."

"Fanta," I said.

"Okay," she said.

"Guys! I knew there was something I forgot to tell you about the new quicksilver formula I made. This one supports you for a day." My mom ran up to us.

"Great job, what modifications did you make?" Luke asked. She pulled out a piece of paper.

"Add much more fizz. And one gram more mercury to the usual five. Add five fluid ounces of alcohol. Five instead of three. And if you usually add sugar, do not, it affects the serum. Also, you need more blood in it. Like an ounce more. And something more radioactive than uranium such as Polonium. Besides, who likes gulping down uranium at the end? Also, for this solution, you add way more salt--like fifty ounces of it. And six milliliters of black mamba venom instead of the usual ten milliliters. A tablespoon of fluorine. Add ten milliliters to the thirty of raw honey. Grind to powder the skin of not one but two golden poison dart frogs. Also, add one tablespoon of vinegar to the usual ten. What else?" She stared down at the paper. "Ah right, the wandering spider venom. I'm surprised we haven't used that yet. Two tablespoons of it. Also the bones of a giant ground to powder. Two tablespoons of it. Though necromancer does it better. Necromancer will do it for a week. But necromancers are so hard to find. Dragon bone does it the best. It will last for two weeks with dragon bone. And no other changes made. The coma only lasts for a day. And with no side effects."

"You better tell Arfaa about your success with the solution of quicksilver."

"First of all, what is quicksilver?" I asked as we neared the front of the line.

"I will tell you once we sit down. For it is too crowded here," my mom said. I got a tray and a glass and silverware and went back to the corner that we were sitting at. Someone tripped me. I fell with a crash. I looked up from the foot to see a boy that looked about twenty. He was sneering at me and all his friends laughed. Hot white anger was building up inside my chest, threatening to explode.

I stood up and said, suddenly very calm, "I'll give you one chance and one chance only to say sorry."

"What will us do Percy?" the boy asked with mock distress.

"Us will say sorry and run away," said the other boy, and all of them exploded laughing. I was just about to slam them each into the wall when an unshaking hand touched my shoulder. I turned around to see Cassiopeia standing there.

"You stay out of this," I said.

"I will once you hear my suggestion. Just leave those stupid blundering idiots to their dinner."

"Fine," I said.

"Hey," one of the boys said, "I'm not a stupid blundering idiot." He was very muscular and he looked about as bright as a turkey.

"You just messed up big-time," one of the other boys said. Everyone looked at them.

"Oh dumbo," she said and smiled sweetly, "you are a stupid blundering idiot because I said that you are." Her face was mere inches away from his and she looked about ready to kiss him. But looks can be deceiving. "And if you ever disagree with me again you are in trouble big-time. As your friend over there said. Consider it a warning this time. But next time, beware." And she leaned in. But instead of kissing him, she kicked his ankle with her shoe, hard, then her fist came up and he flew backward and slammed his head into the table.

"Consider that a warning," she murmured. Everyone in the crowd had looks of surprise on their faces. "Sorry for the mess," she said to the older boy that appeared to be the leader of the boys. She threw him a coin, turned on her heel, and left. I followed her toward our table.

"Why did you give him that coin?"

"None of your business," she said coldly, inviting no more questions.

As we headed toward our table I was able to get another tray and glass. I asked mom, "What was that quicksilver thing about?"

"Quicksilver is a potion that makes you stronger, faster, smarter, and more flexible. If you take the potion you will be more powerful for one day but for the next day, with my formula at least, you will be knocked out. But for mine, there are no other side effects."

"Then why didn't you give it to me when I fought Naquinn?" I asked Luke.

"Because, first of all, it would weaken you for the rest of your life, second of all, we didn't have enough of the potion, and lastly, you would get knocked out for a month instead of a day on your mom's formula and if you are out of commission for a month and Rahmal attacks, we all die. You have to understand this, Magus: Rahmal is ten times stronger than Naquinn."

"Okay, but if I had died in my fight with Naquinn, you guys would have all died too. Don't pretend that I didn't see Naquinn hold off the dragons with one hand while holding off Andromeda with the other hand. He and his army outnumbered you five to one. Who knows how many those giants can kill before they die?"

"You are right, but it will make you slower and weaker physically and mentally."

"Okay. Can I see your formula, mom?"

"Okay," she said and handed me the

notebook she was carrying. Inside, the formula read:

- 19 cups of water
- 11 tablespoons of vinegar
- 2 tablespoons of Brazilian wandering spider venom
- 1 tablespoon of fluorine
- 40 milliliters raw honey
- 12.6 grams per liter of carbonation
- 6 grams of mercury
- **5 fluid ounces of alcohol**
- 3 teaspoons of your own blood. Dragon blood works better.
- 3 grams of liquid polonium
- 6 milliliters of black mamba venom
- 2 ground skins of golden poison dart frogs
- 2 tablespoons of giant bone ground to powder. Necromancer does it better, dragon does it best.

Note: If you use necromancer bone it will

last for seven days. If necromancer bone is combined with dragon blood it will last eight days. Dragon bone will last two weeks. If you use dragon bone along with dragon blood it lasts three weeks. If you use dragon blood it lasts three days.

Regular potion lasts for one day with one day of sleep. Scientist, Hope Cobra.

"How did you find all those ingredients?" I asked. "Especially the polonium."

"I have my sources. Lots of children of nature work in labs. Some are snake milkers."

"How did you get three tablespoons of your own blood?"

"Did you notice how sometimes when you got back from school I was very tired?"

"Yes."

"That was from the loss of too much blood."

"How did you experiment with it?"

"I first did it on rats and then when it was successful I tested it on some of the human spies for Naquinn that Arfaa captured. Some of them died. Some of them got weak. Only this formula worked. The person who took it was as strong as ever."

"That's why I could swear I hear screaming in the middle of the night."

"Yes. Because the test subjects were terribly behaved."

"I'm going to eat now," I said, "so how do I do this?"

"First you say what you want for protein."

"Steak medium rare."

"Next say what you want for vegetables."

"Cauliflower."

"What do you want for wheat?"

"Mac and cheese."

"What do you want to drink?"

"Fanta with ice."

"Now say the word abracadabra and everything you want will be on the dish."

"No way. Abracadabra." Instantly the air shimmered in front of me and from it, a piece of steak fell into my tray on a plate. A smaller plate of cauliflower fell onto my tray followed by a bowl of mac and cheese. Then, my cup began to fill with orange-colored liquid followed by a few ice cubes.

Lastly, a folded napkin and silverware fell into the tray, followed by a straw sticking into my Fanta. Then I dug in with all my strength.

The food was delicious. It was even better than the food in my dream. I finished it quickly because I was thinking of Naquinn's breastplate and all the things that I could use it for. So I left the dinner table and slipped into the night. The night air was chili but luckily I had borrowed a windbreaker from the hospital. I heard all sorts of animals--some earthly and some that were probably native to Eldresdore. As I remembered from the dream, I saw the bushes off to one side. There were flutters of wings. I felt every beat against my skin. I felt the breeze, every whisper of it. I felt like I could grab the wind and have it lift me up. So I did. It lifted me up. I manipulated the wind so that it formed a cushion under my feet. I was up in the air hovering nine feet above the ground before I even noticed that I was above the ground. I looked down to see nothing but air below me. That's when I panicked. I lost all control of the cushion under me and I fell right into the bushes. I bonked my head into a branch and the last thing I saw was two big yellow eyes hissing, "Issss it good to eatsssss?" Then I blacked out.

10. The Snakebite

The first thing that I noticed was the smell. It was terrible. It smelled like rotten eggs mixed with old socks. Then I heard hissing. I opened my eyes and saw snakes everywhere. We were in a cavern with bushes for the ceiling. There were arrow tunnels built. The snakes surrounded me, all flicking their tongues in and out.

"It'ssss awake," one particularly big snake said.

"What should we do with itssss?" asked another one.

"Issss it good for eatsing?"

"Wait," I said, "I'm not good for eating."

"We shall have to tessstsss it," another one hissed.

"Good pointssssss."

They closed in on me.

"Don't," I warned, "I am powerful. If you come too close I will zap you."

"What doesss sssap mean?"

They kept closing in on me.

"If you get too close I will have to kill you."

They kept coming.

I fried one of them with my yellow energy. That just agitated them.

The other ones kept moving toward me. I swept the room with my energy. I zapped most of the snakes in the room. The rest of them lunged at me. I killed most of them but one managed to nick me on the back of my palm with its venom gland. I killed the rest of them but could feel the venom going into my blood. I needed to get out of here fast.

I searched the narrow tunnels desperately for the breastplate. I found it with a big portion of the sword and the breastplate that was Naquinn's and was peppered with holes just as I was about to give up. I grabbed them, stuffed them in my jacket, ran toward the ceiling bushes, willed the cushions to pull me out, and sprinted toward the castle that was not very far away. I stumbled into the hospital. I got a nurse and showed him the mark on the back of my hand.

"A snake gave this to me," I said.

"I do not know what type of snake it is," the nurse said, "I will get a professional doctor who treats snakebites."

I waited, and waited, and waited, and waited, and waited. It was taking such a long time. Just as I was about to lose my patience the nurse came back and said, "this is D.r Quincy, he is our professional recognizer of snakebites." He stepped to reveal a young man.

"Hi my name is Dr. Quincy, I am the blinding light's professional recognizer of snakebites. Do you have a snakebite you want me to recognize?" he said in a monotonous voice. Obviously trying to sound professional.

"Yes, I do."

"Where?" he asked in his monotonous voice.

"Here," I said and pointed at the back of my hand where the skin was starting to turn purple. "I don't know if you recognize it because it was only a scratch."

He glanced at it, got a plastic cup and started chanting as I watched drops of the venom appeared out of thin air and dripped into the cup. After he got a few drops in, he stopped chanting and inspected the liquid. Then he started chanting again and the viscous brown liquid simmered, disappeared, simmered, and disappeared. It kept repeating itself eight times. After the eighth time, a look of horror came across D.r Quincy's face and when he spoke his voice lost all its professional quality. "This is not good," he muttered under his breath. The first hint that I got was that it was either a common not-so-venomous brownstripe or maybe a blackmouth nosok or maybe, just maybe a basilisk." The doctor gasped.

"The common not-so-venomous brownstripe doesn't sound so bad," I said.

"But then I narrowed it down the common not-so-venomous brownstripe and the basilisk. I narrowed it down, again and again, I got the common not-so-venomous brownstripe and the basilisk. I did this eight times but only on the last time did I realize that there was no hope that it is a common not-so-venomous brownstripe and then I knew, knew instantly that the basilisk Hope killed, Siskilinth Naga, Naquinn's pet was not the last basilisk, and that you were bitten by a basilisk," he said. The doctor had mysteriously disappeared.

"But the ones I saw were small, not humongous like Naquinn's pet. The ones I encountered were about thirteen feet long, " I said and thought back to my dream.

"They grow to be as large as Siskeilenth over time. The ones you encountered were about twenty years old."

"My other question is can you heal basilisk venom?"

He shook his head sadly and said "the only known cure is in the Lost Lands it is something called yucuas bloom. You came here too late for amputation and I can postpone your death for a month."

"Fine, then do it. Postpone my death for a month. After this battle, I am going to the lost lands to get yucuas bloom myself."

"Only one problem. You need me to come with you to get the yucuas bloom because I have developed a sense that acts like a homing pigeon. I can sense where the blossoms are the only other person in the blinding light that can do this is Andromeda. I will now make your life longer."

And he started chanting. After he was done chanting he said

"And one last piece of advice: do not trust Luke. Arfaa doesn't trust him. But he should have banished Luke a long time ago. Andromeda respects him for saving her life back in the first battle against Naquinn but now even she doesn't completely trust him." With that, he slinked back through the door and left. That left me with a very big predicament. First of all, should I trust Luke? Or should I not believe the doctor? And most importantly I was dying in one month I would be dead. So searched in the depths of my mind for Pegasus. I found his mind and told him everything that had happened from the dinner, to the snakes, to the blade and breastplate to the basilisk, to the venom, to the cure. He was almost scared half to death when I told him that I was going to die in one month. He said that he was going to get me to Arfaa to get me a room. So I waited for him to fly me to Arfaa. After a few minutes he landed in front of me and scolded me for almost dying, and after that, he said that he was going to try to sense Arfaa's mind and eventually locate where he is and find you a good bed to sleep in for some well-deserved rest. As I waited for him to find Arfaa I looked at the sword and the breastplate. The breastplate was peppered with holes. I switched my gaze to the sword that I held in my hand. It was a giant piece. Most of the sword had survived the blast; the tip was gone but I was sure that they could reforge it.

Then I said to pegasus, *when we get there I will ask arfaa to remake this sword and reforge this breastplate.*

Okay.

Okay.

I have found Arfaa. He said, *I will take you to him.*

Okay.

Hop onto my back.

I did as he told me to. I wasn't about to try to do the cushion thing again. I was too scared. The last time I did it I almost got myself killed. The last time I did it is the reason that I was dying. In short, I was not going to do it again unless it was absolutely necessary and right now it was not. So I got on to his back and he swooped into the sky. We did not speak to each other on our way to Arfaa. For, I was too busy examining the sword and breastplate that was in my hands. I couldn't see much in the soft glow of the moon other than the fact that the breastplate glowed with a bluish hue and that the sword was virtually invisible in the low light. But I could still see the sword sucking the light into it. The flight lasted about a few minutes. In those few minutes, I felt truly free. It was even better than skiing. The pegasus swooped up and down with the grace of an eagle the night air whooshing past my ears. Then he dived down at a terrifying speed. In those few seconds, I lost my grip around his neck and fell. I was so used to falling that for a split second I didn't realize for a second that there was no pegasus beneath me this time. Then I panicked. I managed to grasp the hilt of the sword but the breastplate slid from my grasp and fell into the trees below me. I tried to pile up the air cushions. It was hard. I did it at the last second before touching the treetops. I stood on the air, frozen by fear, then a white streak shot under me and again I felt the solid surface of the pegasus below me.

"Phew," I said, "that was terrifying,"

Glad you are okay. I am so sorry for dropping you. How did you float up in the air though?

I don't know. It Was probably because of Cassiopeia's blessing or something.

The rest of the ride was smooth and without any bumps for, Pegasus tried not to dive. As we neared a clearing that was far away from the castle. I saw the giant forms of Arfaa and Cavia in the middle of the clearing. Then Arfaa jerked his head up and saw me and Pegasus in the sky he rose to greet us.

What are you doing here? He asked.

"We are here because I got bitten by a basilisk," I said

"What?" Arfaa thundered.

"I got bitten by a basilisk. And I am dying right now," I said.

"Oh no," he said sadly, "it proves that basilisks aren't extinct and that you are dying. I have always suspected that Siskilinth Naga was not the last of the basilisk. Such a shame. That you are dying. I will help you find the yucuas bloom in the lost lands myself. But you need to rest at this moment. I am sorry I forgot to tell you but your room is ready. I will escort you there personally today but after that, you will have to find your way by yourself or go ask the front desk."

"There's a front desk in the castle?"

"Yes on the first tower you will find the front desk."

"How do I find the first tower?"

"Ask someone where it is. Almost everyone knows."

"Okay. Can you reforge this blade?"

"Where did you find that?" he asked sounding bewildered.

"I found it in the den of basilisks where I got bitten."

"A den of basilisks?"

"Yes, I fought them off and got Naquinn's sword and breastplate."

"Give the sword to me," Arfaa said.

"Why?"

"Just give the sword to me," Arfaa said again more firmly this time.

"Okay," I said and gave the sword to him. He threw it away into the forest.

"Why did you do that?"

"I did it because that sword reeked of Naquinn's scent. And second, that was a weapon of pure evil; it will corrupt you until you turn as evil as Naquinn."

"Okay, then it deserved to go into the woods and disappear hopefully forever."

"You are right but we better get going. It is about ten o'clock right now."

We soared off into the night. The air was cool. The wind rushed past my ears, my pegasus was diving again. He wheeled here and there and was having a good time. Pegasus snorted something and quick as a flash he spun around upside down and I lost my grip and fell. Right onto Arfaa's back. "You can communicate with horses?" I asked Arfaa.

"Indeed I can," Arfaa said, dropping down and sailing back up. A movement that made my stomach lurch unpleasantly.

"Why aren't you talking to me through the mind?" I asked.

"Because I did not feel like it," Arfaa said. Dropping like a stone toward the lake and skimming his claws over the shiny surface of the lake. The rest of the ride went smoothly without any more complications as we flew towards the castle as we were on top of the castle

Arfaa said to Pegasus, "here we fly higher and if you look to the west you will see a little cabin in a clearing by a river. The moon was setting but as I saw its last rays I saw a river and a clearing.

We dived toward that clearing. Arfaa breathing fire to light our way as we descended. We landed softly on the grass and I saw a hut made out of stone. It was about as tall as I was and there was a simple stable by the river. The building was about five feet wide and seven feet long. It was all made of stone and looked about as comfortable as a brick. There was a simple wooden door at the opening that creaked on its hinges when Arfaa opened it.

"Do you seriously expect me to live there and my pegasus live in that?"

"Looks are not what they are. You find it very comfortable in there. And so will you, Pegasus lord of the pegasi. I entered the room and was shocked out of my breath. From the outside, it looked nothing like the inside. There were indoor water slides and trampoline elevators leading up to the waterslide. There was even an indoor ski slope that had a lift.

"How is this possible?" I asked this was my dream house there was a stairwell leading up to somewhere it had everything I needed.

"It is possible because of magic."

The technology was amazing.

"How did you get the machinery and stuff I thought machines malfunction in Eldresdore."

"They do, but this was created from your imagination so it won't malfunction." Then I thought of something.

"Should I trust Luke?" I asked.

"What do you mean? Should I trust Luke? Is that what you said?"

"Yes."

"You should make your own decisions," Arfaa said.

And with that Arfaa left and flew away. When I stepped up the stairs and saw roller coasters and cotton candy and when I crossed that room I found a door that was marked. MAGUS'S BEDROOM, I crossed into it and saw a king-size bed, a luxurious bathroom, and a closet that was filled with clothes. I had time to play later but now was the time to sleep. So I got fresh pajamas from the closet and turned off the chandeliers. "Lights out," I said and collapsed on the bed.

11. The Second Battle

I blinked the sun out of my eyes and tried to hide under the cover of the bed but then I thought of the basilisk and my doom so I jolted awake and rapidly blinked my eyes to adjust to the artificial sunlight. I quickly changed into a long-sleeved shirt and sneakers. I found that the sneakers had needles and that you can push them in and pull them out. Then there was a little cap that screwed on and said, hydrogen cyanide here. I opened it and looked into it. The space inside was about half an inch high by some inches long by some inches wide. Was it a container with titanium? For walls. I knew what hydrogen cyanide was. My mom had taught me poisons along with some dirty tricks like slipping some hydrogen cyanide into someone's drink or food. Or some botulinum toxin into their dish. In short, I was an expert with poisons. I even knew the recipe from the top of my head that would make the victim throw up a lot. So I knew hydrogen cyanide was. That was nasty. It'll kill you in a few minutes if the dose was enough. My mom also taught me to fight dirty if you were overpowered. I knew how to creep silently. I knew how to wear a messy all forest color cloak. And most importantly I always carried a "cooler bottle" that was made of titanium so it did not shatter that carried hydrogen cyanide because it was the fastest acting poison and in case of emergencies. It had a lock that could be opened by hand in my pocket. My pocket! I looked towards the pile of clothes that I had taken off last night. I searched my pant pocket for the cooler container containing the hydrogen cyanide and found nothing. I checked the other pocket, and there was the bottle. It was a one inch by two inch by three-inch bottle with a screwable cap. I put my shirt over my mouth and nose and unscrewed the cap. I quickly dumped some of it into the shoe. And dumped some into the other shoe. I did not bother with masks because my mom had always said that I was stronger than most people. I dumped the contents into both shoes. After that, I closed the cap, shook the bottle, and could tell that the bottle was still mostly full. *Good*, I thought, *I still have lots left.* I slipped the bottle into my pocket, put the sneakers on, and used the titanium bottle to push the injection needles in, or whatever they were. Then I rushed off to the stable where Pegasus was. I headed past the roller coasters, the waterslides, and everything else until I reached the door. I opened the door and stepped out into the sunlight. Once I closed the door and locked it, I no longer saw the house but only saw it as a small stone building. I walked toward the small stable and went in. The inside was nothing like the outside inside was a soft glow coming from everywhere at once. I saw hay everywhere I saw a river flowing across the room and on the other side was Pegasus himself. There was no ceiling. Instead of the roof, there was open sky. There Pegasus was standing, his knees locked in position.

Pegasus? I asked with my mind touching his.

What?? Shut up!! I'll kill you!! Oh, it's you, he began in a calmer voice. *I'm sorry about that,* he unlocked his knees and asked me, *are we going anywhere?*

Yes, we are. I need you to get me to the castle, I said.

My pleasure, he said.

Thank you, I said. I got on Pegasus and together we soared out into the morning air. It was chili but not unpleasantly so until he dived down and swooped up. With the wind whistling past my ears I now had second thoughts about not bringing a jacket. Then he did a low dive, swooped down even lower, did a loopty-loop that made me scream, climbed up onto a higher altitude, and dove. He dove straight down toward the river. I'm not kidding when I say straight down. He dove straight down, then at an angle inward so I did not plummet toward my death, and swoop up over the river, his wingtip brushing the clear glittering water below. Then he flapped his wings so that he got to a more reasonable altitude.

Then he asked, *where do you want to go?*

To the castle, I said in my mind. He rapidly flapped his to gain a higher altitude until at last, the castle was in sight. I looked down to see a sight that made my stomach lurch. Below me, I saw that the once huge clearing was now a tiny dot with an even smaller strip of blue. Fear clawed at my insides but then, at that moment Pegasus drew his mighty wings back like a falcon and dove towards the castle at horrifying speeds like an SRS-blackbird. I think at that moment we broke the animal record for diving. I think we even broke the barrier for the speed of sound itself. We plummeted like a rock toward the castle. My only thought in the few seconds of diving toward the castle was,

"AHHHHHHHHH."

At the last second, the great white horse banked, slamming me into him and all the air went out of my lungs and I gasped for more air as my pegasus softly landed on the ground. It took me a moment to realize that we were in the courtyard of the castle. There was not a lot of action in the usually busy castle aside from the people that had STAFF sewn on the back of their shirt, only a few people were sparring in pairs. I walked up to one of the staff and asked, "do you know where the rest of the people are?"

He turned around to reveal that He was Dr. Quincy lifting the heavy crate. "Hi, Dr. Quincy," I said warmly.

"Hi, Magus," he said.

"Do you know where the rest of the people are?" I asked again.

"Yes, I know where they are," he said, "they are still in their beds sleeping. Those are the early risers." he gestured at the sparring group who were now splitting into teams.

"When will the rest of them be here?" I asked.

He checked his watch and said, "they will be here in an hour for breakfast."

"Everybody?" I asked.

"The ones that want breakfast," he said, "also completely changing the subject but did you think over the piece of advice I gave you?"

"What advice?" I asked.

"The advice about Luke," he said.

"Oh that," I said, "Arfaa said, that I should make my own decisions."

"That's all he said about Luke?" the doctor asked.

"That's all he said about Luke," I said, "why should I not trust him?"

"You should not trust him because first of all, they were once one of Evile's best servants, he and his sister, and also Andromeda and Arfaa have found black gaps in his memory full of nothing. You know that if you want to hide things from mind readers a black hole appears?"

"No, but go on with your explanation," I said.

"Anyway as I was saying the holes appeared he said that they were private. Then after he joined the blinding light, top-secret documents started disappearing. The documents did not disappear at the same time, they vanished one here, one there, but these disappearances all happened after Luke joined the blinding light. Even now some important documents disappear. The only reason Luke did not get tortured is because he saved Andromeda's life," he said.

"Do you need help with that crate?" I asked suddenly wanting to change the subject because I needed more time to think about it.

"Thank you," he said, but I do not need help with it. Why don't you get a ride on your pegasus before breakfast is ready. You will know when breakfast is ready," he said.

"How will I know when breakfast is ready?" I asked.

"As I said, you will know when breakfast is ready," he said, and with that, he carried his crate into the castle.

Pegasus, I screamed reaching for him.

Yes, little one? he asked.

Can you take me for a ride? I asked.

Yes, of course, I can take you for a ride as long as you don't freak out.

Thank you, I need a little fresh air to clear my mind and refresh me and talk to put me to my right mind. For now, a flight is just what I need, I said to Pegasus. After what felt like an eternity Pegasus finally picked me up and did his roller coaster thing. This time instead of being afraid, I actually enjoyed it. The ride was fun. But after that, I had more important matters to discuss than the fun ride. I asked Pegasus if I should trust Luke but he said the same thing Arfaa did, he said that I should wait to make my decision. Then all of a sudden I saw unicorns galloping toward us and flying horses gliding above them. The first rider was carrying a flag that had huge gold letters that printed out BREAKFAST FOR EVERYONE and as that flag bearer came closer I saw that it was mom! I saw that Luke and Andromeda were the two pegasus flying beside her also bearing flags that said BREAKFAST FOR EVERYONE. I told Pegasus to fly toward the central flag carrier. Pegasus flapped his wings to gain height. Until he was about two hundred feet above the ground, then he dived.

As we dived down toward the other pegasus I felt my stomach go into my chest and my heart rise into my throat, for we were almost diving vertically toward the other pegasus. I always liked roller coasters but this was different. I had no harness to strap me in and the dropping feeling was worse than any roller coaster I've ever been in. But it was calming for some reason. I felt as if I had taken over the sky by myself. I said hi to my mom, even though I knew the truth now I still thought of her as my mom because she was always nice to me and had taught me everything. We had breakfast with the same trays. I ordered cereal, scrambled eggs, and a bagel with cream cheese. Except for saying good morning to mom, the morning passed with a somber silence weighing down on everyone. We knew that we were going to win but precious lives would be lost defending the castle from the necromancer. Necromancer! I had to ask Luke if he had made the arrows for Arfaa and Cavia. I searched for Luke everywhere. From one side of the castle to another. Along the way, I heard groups of people murmuring to each other as if a dark cloud had settled over the castle. The halls I passed were not lit with golden lights and did not smell like baking pastries. I searched far and wide for Luke but did not find him anywhere in the walls of the castle. So I decided to go into the courtyard of the castle where the walls surrounded us in a triangle shape. The general air in the courtyard was much merrier than inside the walls there were people sparring everywhere there were amazing acrobats performing. One guy was juggling ten throwing knives. He caught one after another and sent them at the bullseye that a hooded and cloaked archer was shooting at. The archer used his arrows to knock them aside and they were sent spinning toward a person who caught them and sent them spinning toward the hooded archer. The hooded archer intercepted most of the knives with her arrows. She caught the last two and threw them toward the target. The knives bit deep in the wood in the bullseye. The small audience clapped. When the performers stepped back and bowed I saw that the girl was Andromeda and that the boy was Luke. After they were finished I asked Luke, "I have two questions, first, did you give Arfaa and Cavia blowguns?"

"That was unexpected," he said, "but I did request them from the forges. They said that Arfaa and Cavia would have the blowguns by sundown."

"Good, my second question is can you explain the rules of capture the castle?" I smiled for the first time today. He told me that the thing was Like a siege. Half of the red troops would attack the blue castle and half of the blue troops would attack the red castle then after they captured the castle they would have to find a flag. After they found the flag they went to their castle and they won. The team captains would choose the spies. They could choose anyone but the other team captain for a spy. They would pull one person at a time to say if they were guilty or innocent. The spy had to help the other team. The only rules were no maiming and no killing. Dr. Quincy will be serving as a referee and medic if anyone gets hurt with the wooden swords. When I played I got to be the other team's, Luke's, spy. Everything was going well until this team's captain, Andromeda thought about me being a spy. Then things started to go wrong. They had tried to capture me but I knocked a few of them and escaped out the window. I had successfully escaped, yes, but I had not found out where Andromeda had hidden the flag. I returned to the castle and told the guard that I had to see captain Luke. He let me in and told me that Luke was going to be on the top of the tower. I raced up the stone stairs two at a time and found Luke conferring with someone. I told him what had happened and told him my plan. We were going to fly through the top of the tower and sneak into the castle while five people made as much noise as they could on the east and west walls of the castle in the bushy forest, yes the castle was that big. Half of the remaining army would sneak through the boulders and try to attack that way and the rest of the army would defend the castle. Luke said that it was a good idea and that he would do it. The plan failed and we fought on but we knew that we had lost. I had lunch that was made up of a Mcdonald's burger, some fries, and lemonade. In the afternoon we got ready for battle. Arfaa flew up to me and gave me some last-minute advice. He said, *once you feel like that you are tiring out do not push yourself and keep fighting, the right thing to do is to just hide and rest for a few minutes then keep fighting. For we can't have you so tired that you are dying. One last piece of advice, if you fly you must watch out for arrows.* And with that, he was gone wheeling back into the sky. Then as I got ready for the battle and got dressed in the armor that Arfaa had given me. Just as I was about to hurry toward my pegasus, "good luck," someone said behind me, I was so startled that I almost backhanded the person who said good luck. I turned around and saw Cassiopeia standing there.

"Good luck to you too," I said and climbed on to my pegasus. I watched as our army crashed into Naquinn's demons. The second battle had begun. And the nightmare was going on all over again.

12. Loss

My pegasus and I lifted into the air as arrows whistled past our ears. As we flew down toward the battle I could see that the giants were having an advantage against the pegasi. I saw Arfaa and Cavia holding blowguns in their powerful jaws scanning the battlefield for the Necromancer and occasionally killing giants with a swipe of their claws. I told Pegasus to drop me in the middle of a ring of giants surrounding a helpless boy that looked younger than me, but you could never tell how old they are just by looking at them. But I dropped down to the ground anyway and found myself fighting side by side with the not-so-helpless boy. Then I could sense two more forms dropping beside me. I looked to the two forms, in the dim light I saw the forms of Luke and Andromeda fighting. We formed a ring with our shoulders and fought like demons. Then I saw another form drop beside us, it was mom. Then mom said to me, "let's see what I taught you."

As if on cue we all broke the formation and with our swords in our hands and charged the giants. I ran up the side of a giant like a gazelle willing the wind to form a mini-tornado around me. I stabbed the giant in the chest again and again until finally, the giant fell, then I moved onto the next giant. Eventually, we were standing in a circle with all seven giants lying dead at our feet. Then a bony figure strode toward us. He lifted his hand and all seven giants got up and strode to his side. Then in a blur of red and green, the giants were all laying dead in front of the claws of Arfaa and Cavia, the dragons had arrived. Andromeda drew an arrow and aimed it at the necromancer, that's when Cassiopeia arrived. She sat on her pegasus, drew an arrow and pointed it at the necromancer. The necromancer just laughed. It was an evil laugh that tore at my eardrums, the archers simultaneously fired at the necromancer. But not before the shuriken left his hands and spun toward my heart. Time seemed to slow down just as the shuriken raced toward my heart. I was shoved away by someone and that someone's body landed on top of me with a thud. I got up and brushed away the blood that was on my shirt. Blood? Where did that come from? I stared into the girl's eyes, Andromeda's eyes and saw that they were oddly blank, and then saw the throwing star sticking out of her heart, and at that moment I was sure that she was dead. My legs gave away and I plopped on the ground and started crying. After that I was told how the battle ended. The unicorns lured the bulk of the army into a U shape in the castle wall and then archers had started firing onto the army. Ten pegasus even dumped lava on the invaders. And Arfaa and Cavia melted some of them. And after they fled children of nature were sent to chase them down. We had easily won the battle.

13. Racing Against Time

The next day as I was preparing to leave and get the yucuas bloom I wondered why Andromeda had used her life to save mine. I hadn't even known her that well. I hadn't even been nice to her. Now I regretted not ever being friendly to her. But now was not the time to regret now was the time to do something. I needed to get the yucuas bloom. So I packed faster frantically shoving things into my pack. It took a few minutes but after I was done my pegasus took me out from the shop on the tower to the clearing below where Arfaa, Cavia, and a few others were waiting for me. My pegasus and I swooped toward the clearing and saw Dr. Quincy packing as well. I said my goodbyes, hugged my mom, shook hands with Luke, and hugged Cassiopeia, and turned to Dr. Quincy and asked, "are you ready?"

"Never been more prepared," he said as he hopped onto his pegasus. I looked back to the tomb of Andromeda. The adventure was over for her, but it was only beginning for me.

14. Epilogue

The white falcon blinked its beady black eyes as the tree branch under his claws swayed with the breeze. He saw the two pegasus and their riders, as his eyes focused, soaring in the chili morning air. He squawked and flapped his wings. It was only a matter of time before they would die, and their corpses lost forever in the Lost Lands. It was time to report back to his master, and his master would have her desired revenge.